Natalie's Notorious National Anthem

Susan Kendall Graham

To order additional copies of this book, contact:
Xlibris
844-714-8691
www.Xlibris.com
Orders@Xlibris.com

ISBN: Softcover   978-1-6641-8348-3
         EBook   978-1-6641-8347-6

Print information available on the last page

Rev. date: 07/12/2021

Natalie's Notorious National Anthem

"Tonight is here already! What am I going to do? I'm too terrified to sing in front of a crowd," Natalie groaned to herself. It seemed as if a cup of popcorn was exploding right inside her stomach. She felt her wet, clammy palms. In just two hours she had to perform her solo.

Crawling under her comforting patchwork quilt, she wrestled about what to do. Natalie shut her eyes so tightly her forehead ached. She heard the tinkling of little bells, and saw purple spots swirling around her bedroom. Voices bounced in her head.

"You're very talented," she heard her parents brag.

"Just concentrate on your breathing," she imagined Mrs. Nuckols saying in music class.

"Oh, Natalie, what are you so worried about? You can do anything," she pictured her best friend, Beth, say.

What if these people were wrong and I stink at this singing business?

Natalie thought a warm bath would help her nervousness. She turned on the faucet in the bathtub. Gardenia fragrance from the bubble bath filled her nostrils. She arranged her concert clothes on the bed. A long black silky dress decorated with silver flowers, black knee-high stockings, and patent leather pumps. The chorus sold candy bars and magazines to purchase these uniforms.

"Oh no," Natalie exclaimed as she saw the dog go into her room.

Six-month old Brody grabbed one shoe and the chase began! Natalie ran to one side of the bed and her black Labrador raced to the other. "Give me that shoe you rascal!" she demanded. "They are brand new." She lunged forward only to land on a pile of dirty clothes.

Brody didn't pay one bit of attention to her and promptly crept under the bed. The shoe dangled from his drooling jaws. Natalie finally caught hold of the heel and pulled. Back and forth, back and forth, they played tug of war. At last Brody relinquished the shoe.

Natalie fell backwards and bumped her head on the trashcan. She felt a knot forming. Her chewed-up shoe had barely enough leather for her foot to fit. Luckily, 321her gown would cover it.

Natalie swung her head around and nearly fainted when she saw the river of water covering the white and pink tiled floor. She hurried to cut off the water only to slip forward into the edge of the sink.

She turned off the water. Blood ran down her brow. Rummaging through the medicine cabinet, Natalie could only find a *Spiderman* band aid. Reluctantly, she applied it. "You call this calming my nerves?" she complained.

"I better clean up this flood before Mom sees it," she thought. It took every terry cloth towel from her linen closet to soak up the water. She tossed the wet towels in the bathtub and closed the shower curtain. She planned to wash them when she returned home.

With a knot on the back of her head and *Spiderman* on the front, she phoned Beth for advice. "When I'm nervous, I always drink a coke milkshake," explained Beth. "I concentrate on the smoothness of the ice cream soothing my throat and it takes my mind off of whatever I am worried about."

Natalie took Beth's suggestion. After dressing, she rushed downstairs to the kitchen and filled the blender with chocolate peanut butter ice cream and coke. She pushed the button but had forgotten to put on the lid. Milkshake sprayed all over the kitchen counter, on the floor, against the refrigerator, and even atop the stove. What a mess! Milkshake splattered on her new performance dress.

"Mrs. Nuckols is going to kill me," Natalie moaned. What was she going to do? Her stomach now felt like an erupting volcano and her hands waterfalls of sweat.

"Here, Brody. Come on boy!" Natalie shouted. She knew the canine vacuum cleaner would lick up all the evidence in just a few minutes. Brody happily lapped up the ice cream covered floor, while Natalie wiped off the appliances. Natalie even encouraged him to jump onto the counter to finish the clean-up.

"Let's go, Natalie," called her mother from the front door. "We have to be there in 15 minutes." Natalie quickly grabbed her coat so her parents wouldn't notice her milk-stained dress and torn shoe.

"We can't wait to hear our little songbird this evening," boasted her dad while driving the red Honda.

"But Daddy, I'm too nervous for anything to come out of my mouth." She began visualizing what had happened before leaving. She chuckled to herself and laughed right out loud thinking about the shoe chase, overflowing tub, and splattered milkshake. For a minute she forgot her nervousness, but only for a minute. Nothing helped!

They arrived at Memorial Middle School. Natalie's Mom and Dad threw their arms around her and gave her a huge squeeze. She could hardly breathe!

"You're going to be the hit of the evening," said her mom. Natalie wore her coat until the last minute.

It was time. The chorus finished their warm-ups and lined up to go on stage. The audience quieted down and settled in for a patriotic concert.

Natalie was terrified! She started the whole performance with "The National Anthem." A cappella!

What if I sing flat? Suppose I forget the words?

Trying to forget her fears, Natalie quietly confided in Beth about her adventures at home. The audience began to snicker. When she got to the part about grabbing her coat so her parents wouldn't see, she heard the people laughing hysterically.

"Your mic!" said Beth. "It's been on this whole time."

Mrs. Nuckols gently pushed Natalie onto the stage. She didn't want to see the people laughing at her. She closed her eyes, took a big breath, and began to

sing. Her knees shook. Droplets of perspiration loosened *Spiderman*. A hush spread over the auditorium. She gingerly opened her eyes and saw the crowd fixed

on her every word. The guests were actually enjoying her rendition of "The Star-Spangled Banner." Their attention gave Natalie the courage to hold those high "G's" and smile oh so slightly.

"And the home of the brave," she finished.

Dead silence. Nothing. They hated me!

A few people wiped tears from their eyes. Natalie was shocked. Had she really caused all this emotion? It was only "The National Anthem!" she shrugged her shoulders and outstretched her hands to her sides when the audience started clapping. From the corner of her eye she saw

Mrs. Nuckols motioning her to take a bow. She curtsied and ran off stage. Her teacher embraced her tenderly and requested the rest of the chorus to take their places on the risers.

The concert concluded. Natalie feared the consequences of the messy house and stained dress.

"Great job," said Beth.

"You were marvelous," her parents beamed.

"*The National Anthem* set the tone for the entire concert," Mrs. Nuckols said proudly.

No one had acknowledged the dangling band aid, chocolate-stained dress, or destroyed shoe.

She *did* sing like an angel. She *did* have talent. Natalie had performed without a hitch. Maybe next time her stomach would only feel like a ripple instead of an explosion!

Printed in the United States
by Baker & Taylor Publisher Services